Where Did the Hills Go?

Where Did the Hills Go?

Lali Gupta Chatterjee

Columbus, Ohio

This book is a work of fiction. The names, characters and events in this book are the products of the author's imagination or are used fictitiously. Any similarity to real persons living or dead is coincidental and not intended by the author.

No part of this book conveys views, policies, or confidential information obtained from any agency, institution, or company where the author works or has worked.

Published by Gatekeeper Press
2167 Stringtown Rd, Suite 109
Columbus, OH 43123
www.GatekeeperPress.com

ISBN: 9781642370713
eISBN: 9781642370720

Printed in the United States of America

Sharing Thoughts

Every few years I feel the urge to write another book of fiction with a physics twist. Partly, it's a challenge to myself—whether I can still do this. Mostly, it is a compelling desire to create a new dedication to our awesome cosmos and the incredible activity that goes on at the subatomic level—deep inside matter.

So, amidst the daily routine of weekday work, including many technical documents, I indulged my dream to write again on weekends, and "Where Did the Hills Go?" was born.

But the world of books and publishing has changed dramatically since my other books were published. Many doubts and fears surfaced rapidly! I had not written fiction in over a decade. And then my fiction always has science entwined in it. What is my genre? Would I be able to handle social media and e-books?

I decided to attend a Writer's Conference to explore the era of e-books and print. It was somewhat reassuring to find many others who were also tremulous about sharing their creations.

Returning home, I discussed the elements of my mystery novella with many and was delighted by their enthusiasm. Cheered on by continued encouragement from family and friends—I am sharing my creation and I hope you will like it. I will welcome your input to shape my next book.

Please do read the 'Closing Note' AFTER you've read the story for a peek at the science behind the fiction.

About the Author

Lali Gupta Chatterjee is a physicist and an author. Love of science and a strong commitment to associated expertise have been the driving forces behind a multi-dimensional, scientific career. Lali's professional experience includes managing federal science programs in particle physics, computing, and broader computational science areas; building partnerships and collaborations; science communications and outreach; scientific publishing and editorial leadership; advanced research and teaching in particle/nuclear and related physics; and more than fifty scientific papers focused on particle/nuclear/muon physics and their intersections with astro/atomic/molecular physics.

Lali Gupta Chatterjee

Connecting physics with people and events has been a way of life for Lali and continues to drive her explorations in the world of science-inspired fiction. Her books, talks, and teaching provide a connection between physics and people, fostering understanding of the relationship between science and the surrounding culture. Lali's first science-inspired fiction with a cast of sub-atomic characters was published in 1995 by Roli Books with a foreword by the 1988 Nobel Laureate in Physics, Leon Lederman. Her second book connecting people to sub atomic particles was published in 2000 by Kendall Hunt Ltd.

Lali likes to write fiction with a physics twist as she enjoys her life with science.

Read more about Lali on her website www.storiesbylali.net

Credits

I would like to thank family, friends, and colleagues who have read and cheered early incarnations of this novella when it was a much shorter story—Moinak, Sujata, Anita, Jim, Laura, Guenn, Clair, Ted, Melalie, Ted, and Mithu.

Special thanks to those who have persevered through the longer versions, provided valuable insight, and helped realize this experiment in science inspired fiction that I hope my readers will enjoy.

I also want to thank those who have answered questions and acquaintances who have shared my excitement about this new story.

I would like to thank Gatekeeper Press, Author Connections, and BookHive for their participation in my project.

Contents

Dedication

To all those who encouraged me on this third adventure in science-inspired fiction.

The Headline

Edith was driving to work thinking about her 'to do list' and in parallel recapitulating if she had checked that the twins had everything they needed in their school bags. As she slowed down to stop at the traffic light, she glanced at the news collage on her tablet. What caught her eye was a side headline, innocuously peeping out amidst the stock market, politics, showbiz, and crime. Intrigued as she was by the headline "Where did the hills go?" she had to move on as the signal turned green. But her thoughts remained captivated. How could hills disappear? That's absurd.

Could she sneak a glance at that curious news item? No! One did not do things like that on the expressway—she had climbed the ramp and was winging her way to work, a good twenty over the speed limit. How stupid she was! She could hear the news on the radio. But she was caught in the middle of global economy and weather and must have missed the piece she wanted. Further, the radio did not always cover these little items. Well, she would have to wait to find out about the news item.

For Edith, this day in March 2029 had begun like any other. The usual battle with the snooze button on the alarm, the rush through breakfast and getting the twins ready for school, and finally heading off to work. Little did she think that an unexpected headline would intrude into her daily routine and awaken her curiosity. She wondered if it was just a joke or a ruse by a clever reporter to attract attention. It had certainly captured Edith's! She now wished that she had purchased the voice-activated assistant her car salesman had wanted her to get. Perhaps it would have found her story on the radio. Maybe she should also get a driverless car when her current lease ended—or maybe not. She did not feel comfortable about leaving her life too much in the hands of automation, hence her hesitation in getting the virtual assistant! However, technology had been promising flying cars for several years—and those would be fun if she could afford one! Future traffic solution musings ended as her car pulled into the office parking lot.

Arrival at the office was coupled with the usual rush of impossible schedules and deadlines. Edith worked at a non-profit organization that supported education initiatives in urban areas and had branches around the country. Edith got caught up in the hectic rush of morning tasks and forgot all about the news item. She remembered as she walked down to lunch. Maybe someone else had read about the hills. Salad bowl satisfactorily piled and coffee in hand, she maneuvered between the lunch lines to join her colleagues.

She felt compelled to ask, "Has anyone read about some disappearing hills?" No one had and no one cared. Not even her close friend Joan, who always knew everything. She tried the news headlines on her phone—nothing. The article had probably appeared on her tablet because she had customized her search to pick up unusual items. On an impulse, Edith picked up her bag. She would take a brisk walk. And yes, she would read about that intriguing headline. She collected her tablet from the car and headed out.

The park was very pleasant. The dawning of spring had started a few days back. It thrust probing streaks of color and warmth that were welcome in the aftermath of days of dreary wintry mix. Sunlight shimmered through the budding foliage as, biting into an apple, she finally kept her tryst with the haunting news item.

Where Did the Hills Go?

There were strange reports of unexplained erratic disappearances. Not slow, gradual dwindling, but sudden drastic vanishing. Reporting on one site, the article hinted at more, where geographic landmarks had suddenly disappeared. There were some claims that they just shrank to a small fraction of their original size. The reporter had somehow sneaked out these facts but could not proffer any details or reasons.

Edith could not fathom this. How could real things shrink or vanish? Water could evaporate.

Waists could be shrunk (though with considerable difficulty). Egos could be unceremoniously squashed. But they were talking about land structures like rocks and hills. Apparently, whatever was happening affected a certain area and swallowed or shrank everything in it.

The news story Edith was reading described a remote area in Alaska and was the only confirmed report. A geological survey team conducting experiments on local rocks had noticed the sudden vanishing of a trio of small, connected rocks. The team had marked the area the previous day, prior to measuring the mineral composition. But in the morning, they could no longer find the rocks! It seemed preposterous to Edith as she read on. How could an entire set of rocks disappear? The location was noted in the files. But the rocks just were not where they should be! A concentrated search had revealed what appeared to be the outlines of the rock trio, but no longer as landmark rocks. Rather, they were like inconsequential pebbles fixed in the ground, as if they had just shrunk mysteriously to miniature replicas of their original grandeur.

The scientists were perplexed and at a loss how to explain or record it. They took detailed photographs of the "after disappearance" terrain and compared those photos with earlier records. The pebbles whose shapes appeared to mimic the missing rocks were there in the records but they were not called out, as the conjectures that they were replicas of the hills did not appear to make sense. The formal explanation offered in the report and to queries was one of some sudden geocentric activity—bedfellow of earthquakes and volcanic eruptions but on a much smaller and localized scale. But such activities had not swallowed hills before, with no other notable effects. The reporter did not buy the explanation, but recognized that the scientists or any others he spoke to had nothing better to offer.

Back at the Office

Edith walked back to the office, her mind ensnared by the peculiar news item. She was curious by nature and could not curb her excitement about what she had read. She thought about the beautiful mountains in Alaska that she had seen in so many pictures and how she planned to spend a summer there sometime. She tried to talk to others about the news story as the day progressed. Some lifted their eyes off the computer screen momentarily and some revved up their search engines as they exchanged comments. It had been a relatively quiet afternoon at the office and normally people would have engaged enthusiastically. But it was almost closing time and beating traffic took precedence over curiosity for most, as people were getting ready to leave.

Drew had been working on his new project, happily secluded from the world outside his shuttered office but heard the discussions amongst the few remaining. "What on earth are they jabbering about?" he thought irritably as wisps of conversation intruded into his audio space. He wished they would all vanish like the rocks they were talking about so that he could have his silence back. As the low-level hum of voices continued outside, he could take it no more and confronted his colleagues.

"What is going on? Why is everyone talking so much? Things happen in the world. That does not mean we have to talk or think about them." Drew delivered the dictum with his dour countenance and habitual disdain.

"We are sorry we disturbed you." Edith chided herself immediately once the words were out.

Tall, lean, and uncommunicative, Drew stayed cocooned from the others and Edith knew that is not good practice. Yet, somehow Drew always managed to make her uncomfortable. She did, however, like his British accent.

"Don't let him get to you," Joan rallied, as Drew stormed back to his office. "Drew does not bother me," Joan continued. "I have learned over the years that taciturn people are best ignored."

Joan had dealt with more than her fair share of uncommunicative people. She had worked her way up through merit scholarships and determination. She had learned—but did not like to accept—that women somehow had to work harder and be extra talented to gain recognition that men usually got much more easily. She had degrees in both law and urban planning and brought dual skills to their non-profit organization and was committed to equal opportunities for all.

Edith had had an easier childhood than Joan and had been raised in a family of academics. Both her parents had been professors though in very different subject domains. Edith had learned to value knowledge and critical thought but had neither acquired an instinct for wealth nor a driving ambition for it. Her expertise was education with a focus on content and technology tools rather than process and pedagogy. Edith and Joan had become such close friends partly because they were both idealistic. They liked working at their not-for-profit organization and believed strongly in their mission.

Jake and Edith

As she drove home, Edith kept the radio on. It was amazing how much can change in the time frame of an afternoon! The story had now gone viral and all the radio channels had picked up the news of the weird phenomenon. There were hints of more sightings too. No one seemed to quite know what was happening.

She walked into the house still preoccupied with the strange news item. Jake was home before her and she shared with him the mystique surrounding the vanishing rocks. She wondered why he had that amused air as if he knew something about this. Of course! The airplane engine company where Jake worked had a department that investigated unexplained phenomena. He must know more than he was letting on!

"You knew and didn't tell me?" Edith was shocked and wanted all the details.

"I heard about it in the afternoon," Jake responded. "We do not have any ideas what it means yet," he continued, as Edith queried more about the weird phenomenon of disappearing or shrinking hills.

They checked in on the twins doing homework—seemingly oblivious about the weird news item. Comfortable in the apparent focus of Eddie and Sarah in their assignments, Edith and Jake made supper together that day. Their shared curiosity—bordering on fear—remained unspoken. The uncertainty weighed on them, softened by the empathetic compatibility they had acquired over the years.

Jake told her as much as he could about what he knew without breaching any boundaries of company confidentiality. He always enjoyed their friendly banter and shared congeniality. Edith herself had completely forgotten her occasional peevishness about her clockwork-style lifestyle that left her little time to have fun and enjoy relaxing with the family. Her curiosity, toned down with streaks of anxiety, was focused on the strange phenomena of disappearing hills. The news item had taken over her conscious mind as she tried to process everything she had read about global disasters in history.

Framed by their large kitchen window, the moon peeked out from behind the clouds, flanked by a few other stars. It seemed far enough away to be safe. But who knows?

"Do you think the moon could have vanishing zones too, if all this is real?" Edith's question caught Jake by surprise. He had become a trifle diverted from the news of the day as he was focused on checking if the meat was done.

"I hadn't thought of that. It could be happening anywhere, I suppose, whatever it is," he replied.

The Twins Knew

Edith and her family lived in Virginia in the western suburbs of Washington, D.C. Jake worked downtown and Edith's work commute took her further west to Herndon, VA. Jake was usually able to get home earlier and leave later in the morning. However, Jake also often started dinner and Edith loved that! They had friendly neighbors and had lined up a few child sitters so the children could come straight home from school. The sitters also took Eddie to his weekly tennis lessons and Sarah to her science club.

So much for Edith and Jake's complacence that the twins had not heard! They had indeed heard about the disappearing hills in school. In fact, they were both writing about it as part of their homework essay. Eddie was a fan of vintage *Star Wars* movies and all science fiction; his projections were all about aliens annihilating the hills. Sarah was more rooted in today's science and proposed chunks of antimatter were annihilating the hills. Edith wondered why it had taken people at her office so long to hear the news story about the hills, when it seems even the children had heard in school. Maybe their teacher was curious like Edith and had a customized search engine like her own.

Jake and Edith were somewhat relieved that the children were animated and looking for causes rather than being apprehensive about the unknown. Taking their cues from Sarah and Eddie, they too joined the discussions and the debates between the two proponent theories and added ideas they had heard.

Jake proposed some more down-to-earth causes rather than aliens or antimatter: "What about some kind of earthquakes or landslides?"

It seems the twins had already discussed and moved on from such mundane options while at school. Their teacher had said there had been no reports of seismic activity or landslides. Both Edith and Jake smiled with reassurance that their children were in a good school and learning in interactive ways.

"You still have to eat your vegetables," Jake reminded Eddie, who was trying to hide them on his plate. Reluctantly, Eddie complied as Sarah brought up the favorite topic of Granddad as the conversation returned to the news of the day. A discussion on science and possible explanations for the hills disappearing would not be complete without input from Granddad.

Granddad (JD)

An august and distinguished doyen of science since the previous century, Edith's dad, JD, had tired of the relentless publish-or-perish driver of science that left little time for thought. After retiring, he had moved back to their family home in Connecticut. It was like old times when Edith and Jake took Eddie and Sarah home to visit with JD and Edith's mother Molly. Molly had also formally retired but continued to write for various magazines and occasionally taught a freshman class in philosophy.

The oak tree still harbored fond memories of JD explaining about the falling apple that alerted Newton to the laws of universal gravitation. The windows in Edith's grandfather's library had been enlarged to transform it to JD's study, and JD's physics books and models of experiments glowed in the afternoon sunlight. His father's collection, built over decades of studying anthropology, had been preserved but relocated to the basement where its late owner still reigned over it via a life-sized portrait.

Their family associated the small pool in the yard at the back of the Connecticut house with Archimedes and flotation, one of the stories her father had told them amidst BBQ wings on a summer evening. Unconsciously, Edith's face lit up with a smile as she thought about ancient Greece and the curious scientist streaking down the streets shouting "Eureka!" meaning "I have understood." Archimedes had understood how objects float and this would eventually seed the technology behind ships and planes.

Whether as a child or as an adult, Edith had never tired of hearing JD explain science. He could share difficult concepts with a comfort that comes from true knowledge. Well-known for his popular expositions on science, he sometimes wore his Einstein mask to explain science and share the example of how Einstein had combined what some might consider a tedious office job with creative, groundbreaking discovery.

JD had become somewhat of a recluse since he retired, though he continued his deep engagement with physics, which was his specialization in science. He was always happy to talk with Sarah and Eddie and was probably responsible in part for their love of science. They both enjoyed going to the lectures where JD demonstrated rainbows and sunsets inside the lecture hall. They all had learned a lot about atoms and matter just by talking to JD. They also heard about the amazing world of sub-atomic particles—hidden from, and yet embedded in our own.

Questions Abound as the News Spreads

The audio and visual media were inundated the next day, Day 3 since the first observation. Unconfirmed rumors filtered in from other places, other countries, other scenarios. The news item Edith had seen—one of the first leaks acquired by an enterprising and determined press—was now lost in the chaos.

Conversation at the lunch table in Edith's office veered to the disappearing hills. "Did you hear that aerospace checks have revealed larger missing peaks and apparently shrunken hills amongst the major mountain ranges?" asked Joan.

"Yes," a colleague responded. "Global satellite scans have also exposed significant distortions from previously recorded topographical earth surface maps in select areas."

"The locations and positioning of the affected sites seem to have no correlation and are sprinkled erratically over the globe. What possible cause could there be for such inexplicable phenomena?" continued Joan.

"Sometimes it reminds me of planes disappearing in the Bermuda Triangle," said Edith as she joined the conversation. "But it seems we still don't know if things are disappearing or shrinking!"

"Yes. It seems totally crazy!" Joan agreed. "The

residual boundaries and remnants sometimes appear to display memory of the original structures adding credence to the 'shrinking' hypothesis rather than disappearing."

Governments and leaders in most nations were as perplexed and bewildered as the general population and were trying to ascertain the threat level. This was hard to do as its reason was completely unknown, as well as where it would strike next. It was not like tracking a storm where experts could chart a projected path and predict regions in danger. It was not a health epidemic of any known kind because officials still did not know about individuals or groups who may have been swallowed along with the land they were standing on. The normal categorizations of disasters and threats had become irrelevant in the face of this invisible monster.

It Becomes Personal for Drew

The person who brought up the matter next in Edith's office was, strangely, Drew. His cousin

Julian had been hiking in Asia and had been close to one of the hills that had mysteriously shrunk. Drew did not like Julian much, but then there was hardly anyone Drew admitted liking. Nevertheless, he was listening, somewhat superciliously, as the family had put Julian's call from Asia on speaker. Julian was Drew's cousin on his maternal side and was a charming and jovial personality loved by all. He combined mathematics and mountain climbing in his repertoire of skills and had been hiking in the low-lying hills near the borders of Nepal and Tibet. As with most remote foothills, the area was desolate with scant vegetation. Sherpa guides and adventurous climbers supplemented the occasional dispersed habitants.

Julian's usual happy voice was anguished in the frightened recount of the day's events. Julian had stopped to drink water before he and his Sherpa guide headed back to base camp and he was admiring the beautiful snow-capped peaks in the distance. There was a particular set of three peaks that glittered like diamonds as the frozen flakes reflected sunlight in multiple directions.

The peak on the left was particularly eye-catching as its outline was like a trapezium and reminded him of geometry. As he closed the cap of his water bottle and looked back up, the peak on the left had disappeared! One minute it was there and then . . . it was gone!

As he raised his binoculars and scanned the field of view, Julian saw everything was unchanged except the missing hill. It made no sense and he thought he was hallucinating. He turned to the guide and queried in broken local dialect whether he had noticed the odd-shaped peak and what could have happened to it. Perplexed, the guide reaffirmed that the peak had indeed been there and just as surely was no longer there. It had not become any colder but shivers ran through both hiker and guide as, subdued and scared, they increased their pace back to base.

Julian had heard only vaguely about the news headlines that dominated most conversations of late as he had been out hiking for over a week. Cell reception was still spotty at base camp and television was non-existent. He did not want to wait for the next train into town and hitched a ride to the nearest hotel to get more information and talk to family. Julian's mother wanted him to fly home immediately but others cautioned about the safety of flights during these traumatic times. Everyone was visibly shaken but had no explanation or solutions.

Drew listened in disbelief and horror. The supposed disappearing or shrinking land zones that Edith and others were talking about in office had suddenly become real and personal. As he listened to his cousin's recount of the events and sensed the raw fear and shock in Julian's voice, Drew's veneer of perpetual self-importance crumbled. Back at the office, he shed his arrogance and joined Edith and others in discussions. He even proposed that they suggest to senior management that their non-profit organization consider joining the efforts to help combat this global threat.

People in the office were too busy dealing with what was happening to pay much attention to the change in Drew but they welcomed his transition to fellowship. Joan, who was a rather forgiving person, responded best to the friendlier Drew.

Keeping Family Close

Later that evening back at home, Edith and Jake went for a walk, a piece of togetherness they did not usually make time for these days. Edith told Jake how Drew's cousin Julian had been close to a disappearing site. There was always the fear the phenomenon would affect someone else she knew. She could not understand how Jake could appear unperturbed amid this frightening disaster. Gnawed by her own restlessness and anxiety, she wondered if he just hid his fears better. It was pleasant (and calming) to walk hand in hand with Jake and succumb to the quiet of the star-speckled sky suffused in silver moonlight.

Edith thought about mile markers in their lives as they strolled down the pathway. She remembered how they had met during their last year of graduate school and how it had made the year magical of sorts.

"Do you remember how we went to the Swiss Alps that summer?" she asked—turning to Jake.

"Of course—and we had thought of going to Nepal but never did," Jake replied. "I can't believe one of those hills near Nepal actually disappeared," he concluded and this brought them right back to the present. As if on cue, they both missed the children and retraced their steps back home.

"We should ask your parents to come down and be with us during this time of uncertainty," Jake said to Edith on the way back.

"Likewise, we should call your sister Fiona and see if she can fly out from California," Edith suggested. Fiona was a vivacious and eclectic person who lived her life impulsively and spent most of her time in her tiny house on the west coast. It would be nice to have her cheery presence amidst them, Edith reflected.

The Response Starts

The UN called an emergency Security Council meeting on Day 4. Process, regulations, and resources were always in place and ready for emergencies in all countries. Built and put in place over decades, these are intended to enable fast response to unknown events. In every country, defense, medical, and all scientific personnel were put on round-the-clock alert. But no one knew how to defend against an invisible enemy that appeared to be devouring the world and its future. Politicians, administrators, industry leaders, military, scientists, and economists pooled resources and ideas that looked at a multitude of possible actions. Town hall meetings and impromptu gatherings were springing up in most places as people sought to share their thoughts and fears. The world populace however did not know if anyone could help them. Most people were trapped in a quagmire of disbelief, fear, and anguish that was thankfully topped with an icing of hope as speculations for escape were tossed around.

The scientists and technicians of 2029 were smart, professional, and competent. They knew how to make every sophisticated machinery work. They could detect defects in chips, computer software and hardware in minutes, sometimes seconds. Doctors could diagnose and cure most known diseases. Professionals were assisted in these awesome tasks by a skilled coterie of perfect robots. These robots could manage urban traffic and operate space satellites and networks that handled not only communications but monitored cosmic events as well.

The phenomena of vanishing hills, however, could not be combatted until people knew what was happening. The enterprise of science and technology currently geared to pander to comfort, appliances, and entertainment was hurriedly re-focused on basic research. In the face of a disaster that had no defined location or timeline, humanity did not have the luxury of time to research and reflect in depth. People needed solutions and they needed them right away.

Whether trying to work in the office or running errands, Edith heard the questions everywhere she went. Who or what could be eating up hills? Would it stop at uninhabited hills or envelop populated areas? Questions abounded and rose to a crescendo as they were reinforced from all sides.

Everyone Chimes In

As to be expected, discussions on causes and solutions were not confined to the science and technology communities. This was a challenge for all humanity, for Vanish (or Shrink) did not respect geographical or disciplinary boundaries. There were roughly equal proponents on each side of the Vanish/Shrink controversy. Excited exchanges of thoughts and animated debates ensued amongst an anguished populace clinging to hope and fervent in their will to save the world. Edith and her children along with everyone else tried to comprehend the scientific ideas evolving, sometimes taking sides with various theories.

Jake was walking past a group spiritedly debating transformative technology options over coffee and whether nascent basic research can be accelerated or used as probes.

"Could the science of materials explain where the matter was disappearing?" asked one. "Or could Nano-devices be used to halt the vanishing?"

The answer from the other side of the table was obvious: "How do you halt something when you don't know what it is?"

The group had proponents of the idea that a wandering black hole was mysteriously sucking in isolated parts of the earth. Another, who loved time warps, was convinced hills were disappearing through worm holes! Not to be outdone, an "antimatter" favoring friend piped in: "It could just as well be revenge of all the antimatter that was vanquished in the infant universe and is somehow leaking back in to annihilate our hills."

Jake was smiling as he heard the discussions until his thoughts turned to the reality of the situation that his family and friends and all the things he loved could disappear in an instant. But Jake did not like to indulge in self-pity or feelings of helplessness. His stride became firmer as he focused on what possible channels he could explore to find solutions.

The Phenomenon Takes Over

Schools were still open as were most offices; however, conversations everywhere were dominated by speculation and fear about the horrendous phenomenon. Although the debates about whether hills were disappearing or shrinking were still unresolved, most people and the media were calling it "Vanish" and no adjective could express the distress and dread it invoked. Children—optimistic and creative by their age and natural curiosity—tried to come up with explanations derived from science-fiction movies and space-age futuristic video games, somewhat like the debates Sarah and Eddie had earlier. Various disaster scenarios from cultures across the globe seamlessly transcended social media in its multiple forms.

The inability to do anything made Edith claustrophobic. She called her physicist father, JD, to see if he had any new ideas since the last time she had called—four hours ago! Impending doom had wooed JD to leave his solitude and join with fellow scientists as they tossed around unconstrained theories and conjectures. Besides, he had his family and the grandchildren he loved to think about. They had to be saved.

JD responded to Edith's impatience. "We are all thinking, but we're nowhere near comprehending what is going on. Society has been focused on finances, technology and entertainment for decades. We have not prepared for inexplicable disasters of possibly cosmic origins."

The conjectures and theories were flowing unrestrained now. Time warps, quantum singularities, dark energy, antimatter, worm-hole eruptions, and parallel universes were being enthusiastically discussed. After years of abstinence from wild thinking, those who loved to speculate felt they could do so in their combined attempts to save the earth! But was it too late?

What Can They Do?

Edith reached out to Drew in the office: "Did you ever hear back from management about whether we can initiate any support activities?"

"Not a word," Drew replied. He and Joan were watching a video online about whether cosmic rays or cosmic events could have triggered something.

"That is Leela on your screen!" Edith interjected. Leela was JD's student and a distinguished scientist in her own right. Edith knew her well as a dedicated and inspiring physicist who traveled the world almost as much as Edith's dad. Edith and Leela had gone to graduate school together in Tennessee, and Leela always stopped by when her travels brought her to the D.C. area. They talked of student days and the twins enjoyed her visits too.

"She knows what she is talking about. Maybe we should talk to her and ask how we can help?" Drew sounded really impressed with Leela's discourse on cosmic phenomena.

Joan was one of those people who did not bear grudges and she had accepted the friendlier Drew more easily than many. She responded to Drew's interest and asked, "Could we work together with scientists perhaps to see how we can help?"

Edith also liked the new softer Drew but not enough to think of him as a friend. However, she offered to arrange a meeting with Leela even though she was out of the country on travel. "Why don't you also call your cousin Julian?" she suggested to Drew. "Maybe we can get some more information on how things are holding up in a zone where we know Vanish has attacked. We could set up a volunteer working group whether we hear back from management or not. We can work with other groups to plan what we can do to address the new and inexplicable threat."

At home, Jake too had abandoned his veneer of

calm and was avidly following every new possible solution as each emerged. He joined Edith, Joan, and Drew in their efforts to convene a volunteer group to combat Vanish with the help of Leela and JD. JD and Molly were now staying with them as they had given in to Edith and the twins' insistence to join them. Molly was not thinking about philosophy, which had been her favorite subject and livelihood for decades, but just wanted to be close to her loved ones and recap the science she had imbibed just being around JD for so many years.

Efforts Continue and Diversify

Jake proposed using his expertise and connections in global communications to encourage easier and increased dialogue between scientists and government officials at the international level and at the United Nations as well. Further, his engineering background and his company's proficiency in industrial technology gave him access to additional contacts and knowledge. While Jake appeared calm externally, in reality he was scared inside and felt curled up like the time warps some reporters were referencing to describe Vanish. He felt he had to hide this from others so that he would not add to the general fear all around. So, he did what he did best and kept searching for solutions.

Julian, meantime, had come to grips with his experience and sometimes the adventurer in him felt excited that he had witnessed an incident of Vanish. However, most of the time he was just horrified as he recalled his line of sight admiring and suddenly losing the trapezium-shaped mountain peak. He had managed to find a flight home to the relief of his family and he joined the volunteer group. They planned to work with the various global "big science" experiments and multinational industrial giants that had distributed global networks to facilitate scientific and technical deliberations and the burgeoning ideas.

Jake's communication and outreach had drawn in staff from the United Nations as well as from different political leaders' offices. These efforts added the much-needed dimension of political dialogue critical to implementing activities. But no one had solutions yet nor understood what was happening. People tried to draw on their past expertise and knowledge to seek answers but found none. The optimistic relied on hope that chunks of earth would stop disappearing. The pessimists blamed everyone but themselves for having somehow brought this disaster on the world. Most people were distraught and anxious and felt trapped in an abyss of fear but always scavenging for good news.

Vanish Swallows More

It was Day 5 and Vanish was appalling, horrible and petrifying. Although the number of zones affected was still few, there was more international awareness of the horror. Newspapers, television, radio—all carried their conjured projections of ultimate destruction. Political leaders continued to do what they always did: they talked. Religious fundamentalists heralded the onset of doomsday; its precipitation having been caused by the ungodly lifestyles of sinners. Various cult protagonists tried to seize more power, feeding on the weakness of a terrified world populace. Extraterrestrials were the favorite culprit of many of the media writers, but what possible reason would they have to steal solid chunks of earth? The commercial space flight industry that was the monopoly of a handful of elite corporations tried to boost business by promoting safety in space. These did not gain traction as reports of a missing satellite ruled out nearby space as a celestial zone safe from Vanish.

Unchallenged by technology or ingenuity, Vanish relentlessly spread its hungry tentacles and trespassed into habited areas. Sections of towns were being wiped out as Vanish spread to populated localities. Buildings collapsed in these areas and governments could not evacuate people for no one knew what or where was safe. Panic and fear were pervasive every direction Edith turned. The disappearing zones took with them the people that had lived there, along with their possessions, memories, and dreams. The talk shows asked the obvious questions: What happened to the people as the buildings and trees vanished or shrunk and crumbled to dust? Were they minuscule and alive or were they just . . . gone?

The experts had no answers as miniaturizing or vanishing were not medical problems doctors had faced in the past. As news of missing localities emerged, families and friends from afar sought information about their loved ones. But the local census records in the disappearing townships were lost along with buildings and people. National resources and the workforce were limited in all countries. Most efforts focused on seeking solutions while offering only words of empathy to the grieving. Major records and operations had become digital by the early 2020s, and the loss of computer servers in habited areas struck by Vanish had wiped out many records.

Could people halt this weird disappearance? Would they or their children see the new decade? Confronted with death and a frightening desolate disappearance, humanity craved not the pleasures and comforts they'd thought were indispensable, but just another chance at living.

The household of Jake and Edith continued to function. The unspoken fear bonded them even more closely as thoughts of the sinister Vanish invaded every waking moment. All tried to be brutally cheerful, as people often tend to do in times of extreme stress. To Edith, every moment with the children seemed a treasure stolen from a frightening future. Every so often, her eyes would well up with fearful thoughts of a tomorrow Vanish might swallow. How she regretted the times she had been annoyed or irritated by what now seemed insignificant events. If she could go back in time, she would cherish every activity that represented life and living. Face to face with the all-pervasive Vanish, every manifestation of nature cried out to be caressed: the sky, the sunset, the flowers, and most of all her beloved family.

The Hypothesis of Shrinking

Huddled together in the living room, Edith and her family watched JD answer questions for the media. Several schools of thought were converging on the hypothesis that Vanish was really a super-shrinking instead of a disappearance. Motivated in part by the early reports when hills seemed to have become pebbles, aerospace and geographical information science experts tried to image the resulting terrain from zones of Vanish. Comparison with past maps and records favored remnant forms that aligned better with a Shrink explanation than Vanish. But shrinking was even harder to comprehend than disappearance.

The reporter wanted to know about the shrinking hypothesis that had been proposed to explain Vanish. "What does it mean when something shrinks? Is it like a balloon collapsing as it loses air?"

"An interesting analogy!" JD replied. "Objects around us have sizes determined by their basic building blocks: their atoms and molecules. If the atoms were to shrink, the objects would do so too."

"How can atoms shrink?" the reporter queried.

"Atoms are mostly empty space like the space that fills the cosmos between the stars and planets. This empty space is called the vacuum. One might say electrons define the boundaries of individual atoms. Since two electrons cannot live in the same spot, accommodating electrons gives size to their atomic homes." JD was enjoying himself and the family was watching; their eyes locked on the TV.

Eddie and Sarah ran to their study room and brought back the model of an atom that Grandad had given them. It was made of soft plastic but not moldable. They both looked at it as they followed the TV show that had guest experts from around the world.

"The size of an atom also depends on the properties of the electrons," JD continued. "For example, if individual electrons were heavier, all atoms would be smaller as would the objects they comprise. Somewhat like your balloon, the empty space inside the atom would be squashed."

Despite their attempts to try to squash it to understand how it could shrink, the toy atom Sarah and Eddie were examining would not budge. The twins had to resort to imagination and hand motion to picture how it might become smaller. Granddad's comment that an atom would naturally shrink if the electrons become heavier was intriguing to the young minds of Eddie and Sarah.

The reporter too was persistent. "Can you tell us of any examples of miniscule atoms?" she asked.

Leela, who was participating from Japan, took on

the question. “The best example might be muonic atoms where a particle called a muon replaces an electron. The muon is heavier than an electron and, as JD just said, this makes the atom much smaller. In fact, if electrons were as heavy as muons, all atoms would be much smaller and it might look like Gulliver’s Travels to the world of Lilliput.”

“Wow!” The reporter had not heard of muonic atoms before or for that matter about muons and pondered this new wealth of information. While the reporter would have loved to pursue the muon angle, they had run out of time and the show concluded with the promise of another discussion soon.

The Global Partnership

The sun dawned on Day 6 as JD and his fellow scientists round the world continued to debate ideas amidst mounting panic. It was a coordinated global effort utilizing every available video and teleconferencing network. The volunteer group started by Edith and her colleagues had become an integrated player in the global network of similar volunteer groups. They facilitated discussions, research, and actions. Theories became bolder and more adventurous and were tossed across the airwaves, mimicking a virtual volleyball game where the prize was a saved world!

Amidst the chaos and the pressures of time, ideas began to coalesce along cohesive, albeit nebulous threads. All of these ideas had been discussed in the media and amongst the interested public. Now they took a more serious turn. One track seriously pursued the ideas of spontaneous formation of mini black holes that had reached earth and were swallowing chunks of matter. How could such erratic seeding and feeding of black holes happen? Would such black holes ever be satisfied? Would they coalesce and gobble up the entire world as they knew it? The competing view contended that it was chunks of antimatter rather than mini black holes that had wandered over from space and were annihilating the hills. Proponents of this model argued that antimatter that had been suppressed since the infant universe became dominated by matter was escaping from wherever it was hiding and annihilating our world—section by section.

However, none of these ideas could explain the numerous reports evidencing that while objects and structures were vanishing from sight, they were really shrinking and not disappearing. No one had actually ventured into affected sites to test the residual rocks or soil for fear of triggering new activity. So, they relied on aerospace observational data that certainly seemed to favor Shrinking. The Shrink theory ruled out both black holes and antimatter as the culprits and provoked other creative ideas of what might be happening.

Governments, bureaucrats, and law enforcement agencies around the world were at a loss what to do. Their usual plans or back up plans for disasters could not be applied. Where do you evacuate people? There was no point in imposing curfews. People were not protesting or engaging in unlawful activities. They were just scared beyond words. Politicians and leaders continued to try to reassure people but they were not feeling so reassured themselves. Unanimously, people around the world turned to the science and technology experts who were trying to brainstorm causes and solutions. Bureaucrats and politicians stepped back from trying to impose rules and provided support to the science and technology enterprise. The United Nations tried to ensure that all nations worked together and supported the global partnerships led by scientists trying to unravel the situation.

Edith's Home

Edith and her family were as frightened and dazed as everyone else. Edith was relieved that JD and Molly had moved in temporarily and that they could be together while facing this unknown phenomenon. Jake's fun-loving sister Fiona had also moved in. She had been in nearby Pennsylvania when Jake called and readily agreed to detour to Virginia at this time of travail rather than return to California. Fiona was different from Jake; she was fun-loving and unpredictable and not so organized. While Fiona was not having fun anymore, she was trying to keep hope and optimism alive amidst the feeling of doom. And Jake, too, was not that calm anymore!

Schools were not open for classes but classrooms were being used for planning and volunteer groups to meet. In fact, Jake was running international communication operations out of the twins' school to facilitate agencies to share news and updates, and Edith and Drew's volunteer group was managing a rapid response hotline. The problem was no one had answers and could only offer empty reassurances that they themselves could not fully believe. Edith did not want to leave her children for a minute and felt relieved that they enjoyed listening in on Grandad's scientific discussions so much and adding their own imaginary tweaks.

It was early evening and the family was going over events of the day and taking a break from constant news on television. Molly marveled that people were working together and bureaucrats were actually letting scientists and technology professionals lead the search for solutions. J.D. commented, "It is equally remarkable that the scientists are not quibbling over who is right but trying to work together!"

"I think this is all happening so fast that carpet baggers have not had time to emerge as they did during long wars of the past," Edith commented.

"I did read somewhere that some scam companies have emerged trying to sell safe zones," shared Fiona. "But I think people are listening to the warnings being disseminated widely."

Edith went and sat next to Eddie and Sarah where they were playing video games. Jake joined her. Fiona gazed fondly at them and took some cozy family photos. Molly and JD looked at each other, overcome by complex feelings of joy and gratefulness for their wonderful family as well as the dread of what the next day, or just the next hour, might bring.

That night the children fell asleep in the living room. No one had slept much of late. Jake carried them to their rooms and mother and father both lovingly tucked them in. What do you do in the face of a disappearing tomorrow? Closing the door behind her, Edith brushed away her tears. Snuggled in Jake's arms, she just wanted to be close to him as love, emotion and fear overwhelmed her.

Edith and Fiona go out of Town

In the midst of the craziness all around, Edith was assigned to a meeting about a hundred miles out in the nearby hills. Loathe to leave her family during uncertain times, she was able to juggle schedules and arrange to reschedule her presentation to the morning of the first day and participate remotely for the other days. She no longer fought her battles with the alarm clock in the mornings as waking up meant more time to spend around her home and with her family. As dawn was usually earlier, she often watched the soothing streaks of pink and red splash across the sky before starting her day.

Fiona had offered to accompany Edith on her trip that day. Being a morning person and accustomed to running or trekking around her tiny house in warm California, rising early to join Edith was no problem for Fiona. She planned to hike around the meeting place, take photographs, and absorb some local culture while Edith had her meeting; she would also take the wheel on the drive home.

Both women had been quiet in the car driving

out. Everything looked so beautiful with the soft blush of dawn brightening to a vibrant orange before becoming ablaze with the bolder golden yellow as the sun climbed atop the hills. The canvas of color heralding the new day seemed oblivious to the trauma consuming the world populace as they struggled with Vanish or Shrink.

Fiona reflected on her life in California, her job as a photographer and her hobbies of painting and sketching. These last few days with Jake and his family had been pleasant, even with the scepter of Vanish hanging over them. Perhaps she should think about relocating to be closer to family. Jake and Fiona had lost their parents early on and were very close though they lived at opposite ends of the country. In principle, Fiona's tiny house could be moved, but she also thought about how much she liked living in California. She settled on the obvious compromise: she would spend more time in VA and would make sure Edith, Jake and the twins visited California at least once a year.

"Let's meet in the lobby around noon," Edith said as she went into her meeting.

“We can have a quick lunch at that cute café with the patio before heading back,” Fiona responded.

Fiona walked over to some children playing near a sculpture that cast shadows of various shapes augmented by the children striking different poses. Fiona never had problems walking over to unknown people and chatting with them. She thought about how different she and Jake were in this regard. Jake was reserved and rarely spoke without thinking, and unlike Fiona, he usually had to be prodded to exercise. Still, Fiona thought he had always been the world’s greatest brother and she was close to everyone in his family. As she took photographs, Fiona thought about their childhood spent in Europe and the changes in lifestyle when they had moved to the U.S.

Ambling over to the cafe, Fiona found a comfy spot and took out her sketch book to capture the view with her pen and complement the digital versions in her camera. She went ahead and ordered sandwiches for herself and Edith—so that they could make an early start back. The two sisters-in-law chatted about their surroundings and inevitably the conversation turned to Vanish and how it was eating up hills and changing the topography of the earth.

Edith Encounters Vanish

"Let's get back before dark," Fiona said as she took the keys from Edith and they headed to the car for the drive home. Since Fiona was driving, Edith could look out at the hills around them as she thought eagerly about getting back home soon. She was also thinking back about the meeting and wondering if she needed to call in and listen to the afternoon session or just wait and check in the next day.

Two hilltops about forty-five degrees to her northeast caught her eye. One had a pretty cottage and beside it a rather ugly structure that could have been a giant scarecrow or some natural recycling instrument. The other hill had some cows grazing and she wondered about them being at such a high altitude and assumed there was a cattle farm nearby outside her range of vision.

Suddenly, it happened—right before her own eyes. The cottage, the structure, the cows just disappeared along with the hills they were on. Edith blinked her eyes. She was shocked. She turned to look at Fiona for sanity and then glanced back to the hills. She hoped her field of view would return to normal and the cottage and cows would all be where they were. But they weren't. They were gone. So, this is what people were talking about? This was happening before her own eyes. This was not just a news story. This was not just a report on television. This was her reality.

Forcing herself out of her stupor and shock, Edith turned to Fiona. "Where did the hills go? Where did the cows go? What just happened?"

"What are you talking about?" countered a startled Fiona as she strove to regain control of the car that had swerved. Her eyes had been on the road and she did not know what Edith was talking about and was caught unaware by her question and the fear in Edith's eyes.

Edith was sobbing by now. "The hills over there vanished right in front of me. I don't know why I noticed; they were about forty-five degrees northeast. There was a cottage there and an instrument or something. There were cows and trees. Where did they all go? What should we do?"

Fiona found a shoulder and pulled over to the side of the road. She was as terrified as Edith by now and too distraught to drive. She had not noticed the hills in question and did not know they were gone. She wondered if the continuous threat from Vanish had gotten to Edith and was playing tricks with her. "Are you sure about what you saw?" She asked Edith. "Are you all right?"

"I am not imagining it." Edith was still crying almost hysterically and pointing to the east as they had moved forward since the disappearance. "Do we call 911?" Edith asked. "Should we call Jake and the kids first? How do we get home?"

Fiona was as confused as Edith was and had no experience about this kind of emergency. As if by instinct, she took out her camera and photographed the area Edith was pointing to and then flagged down another car that was passing by.

The people in the other car had been following Vanish closely in the news and comforted Edith. One of them called the police and another called the local news. Fiona and Edith tried to reassure each other and to call home.

The Police Arrive

The police arrived as a distressed Edith got through to Jake. “It’s happening right here,” Edith cried. “I saw the hills disappear. There was a house there, too. What happened?”

Jake could not believe his ears. Until now, this had been happening in other places. It was not supposed to happen near home. It could not happen so close to his loved ones. Even the usually unruffled Jake could not be calm or think of a plan. He was glad the twins were at school and could not see his agitation or hear what their mother was going through.

“I have to talk to the police,” Edith said as she turned the phone over to Fiona. The police pulled up local topographical maps and confirmed that indeed there had been two large hills that had been majestic landmarks and they weren’t there anymore, just as Edith said. They did not have information on habitation or farms handy but did find records of the hills Edith had been looking at.

Jake asked to talk to the police and inquired if they would bring Edith and Fiona home as he did not think they were in any state to drive. He stayed on the phone with them both and put them on speaker with JD and Molly. Fiona had not actually seen the hills vanish and had not noticed them until she saw the pictures the police had found. But for Edith it was as real as it could be. She had been looking at the hills and the little house on one of them and some cows grazing on the other. Before her eyes they had all vanished. She seemed frozen in time at that moment of disappearance as she tried to reconstruct it over and over again in her mind.

"Would you like some water?" the policewoman asked.

Edith shook her head but did not speak. Her life flashed before her eyes: the good times, the not-so-good times, the past, the present, and all of it dominated by visual images of her wonderful children. She thought about the people who might have been in that house. She thought about the cows that vanished and the trees. Turning in agony to Fiona and the policewoman, she shouted again "I can't believe I saw the hills Vanish!"

Edith was shaking, but her frozen silence had broken and tears poured down her face as the dams holding her emotions broke and she started sobbing again. They gave her a sedative to calm her and Edith clutched Fiona's hand as she dozed off in the police car.

Back Home

The children were home by the time the car pulled in and they ran to Edith as she got out of the car. Mother and children hugged as Jake joined them. Molly embraced Fiona and thanked her for staying calm and thanked the police for bringing them both home safe.

JD was watching and grew even more determined to solve the mystery of what was happening and vanquish it. There had to be a scientific explanation of the happenings and a way to stop them. This was too close to home. This was his family, his wonderful daughter and his precious grandchildren. He loved Jake too and he and Molly thought of Fiona as a second daughter. JD could not get over the fact that Edith and Fiona had been caught in the vicinity of a Vanish or Shrink episode and that his daughter had experienced it firsthand.

Back at home with her loved ones, Edith seemed to respond much better to efforts to calm her. The local press had arrived and had questions for them all. Sarah and Eddie were taking it in stride. Relieved that Mom was home, they too were piping in as the reporters talked. Joan and Julian had come over and the room was filled with relief that they were all safe and well, yet enmeshed with the horror of what Edith recounted in her graphic description. The reporters compared Fiona's photos of the zone with past pictures of the majestic heights and the documented absence was unbelievable. For Julian, it was reliving his own experience over again and he opened up to Joan in Edith's kitchen as he went over that traumatic memory from the past.

No one was in a mood to make dinner that evening and all voted to order pizza. As the family tried to recoup, Eddie blurted out an obvious question: "Why doesn't someone really check if things are shrinking or disappearing?"

"Because no one wants to risk going into those places," Jake responded. "They are now cordoned off danger zones."

Children can be persistent. This time, Sarah had a suggestion. "People have drones. Why don't they send drones in to check out what is happening?"

Jake takes Action

Jake stopped abruptly on his way to the kitchen to get glasses. "That is exactly what we should be doing," he said loudly and clearly.

Everyone stopped talking and stared at him. "How would we contact the right people to do that?" Molly asked. "Who decides on such matters?"

Edith suddenly sat up. It was as if everyone was charged with optimism again and the children were delighted that they had provoked the adults to look for new paths.

Jake and everyone forgot about the glasses he was

on his way to get. They all started talking together. Jake had never been so animated before, nor was he concerned that people saw this side of him. "I can talk to some people," he said excitedly. "Maybe the volunteer group can also network."

Jake picked up the phone and went into his study with his laptop. He called his boss and a whole lot of other people. Several video meetings and some hours later, he emerged to announce the good news. They had been able to rush through required permits and were on standby to send drones in the next day to the spot where Edith had witnessed the disappearance. In fact, they were able to get authorization for checks on a few other affected zones as well.

The family gathered back in the living room. Edith had, of course, forgotten to call back into the conference. She and all were energized by the new directions the search for answers was taking. Grandparents, parents, and aunt were all incredibly proud of the smart and resourceful twins. The twins themselves were still assimilating that the grown-ups had actually taken their ideas seriously and acted on them! It promised to be a great story for their friends.

How Could the World be Shrinking?

While Jake and his network of contacts were waiting for answers from the drone-based research, ideas continued to be tossed across the high-bandwidth transoceanic data network lines that had been rapidly transitioned from data flow to communications channels. Proponents of the school of thought favoring Shrink as the cause had invoked the particles called muons because of their ability to make smaller atoms. These muons continued to serve as reference points to understand miniscule atoms if atoms were indeed shrinking.

"But real atoms have electrons, not muons" was the standard irate response from the "hungry black hole" or "antimatter" advocates.

"What if some of the electrons that give size to atoms and everything, have turned into muons, making atoms smaller?" proposed the Shrink protagonists. "Usually muons turn into electrons when they die. Perhaps somehow the opposite is happening and electrons are turning into muons in select areas?"

The key word here was "somehow" because

the "how" could not be ascertained. The scientific community and the wider world populace were open to any and all ideas that could explain and halt whatever was happening.

"Are there any ways in which electrons can turn into muons or just become heavier? What is the connection?" asked a prominent scientist-turned-politician. "Could electrons be getting heavier in certain parts of the world? We have to uncover the cause and figure a way out from the impasse!"

JD could not agree more. They had to understand and find a solution. This was so much more than those scientific research problems that had kept him awake at night for solutions in the past. This was personal and it was real. The very lives of those most near and dear to him depended on success. Just dedication was not enough. The scientific and technical communities of the world must find a solution and they must work with governments and industry to acquire the resources needed to save the world. "IF" something could be done was not an option. They had to find answers and save their world.

Joan and Julian

Back at the volunteer group in Virginia, Joan and Julian had developed a close friendship bordering on more. Perhaps the advent of Vanish with its haunting scepter brought them close. But Vanish was not the only catalyst for this blossoming romance. Edith, who had observed the signs since Julian had joined their volunteer group, had been gently nudging it along by arranging accidental meetings. Entwined in the shared pledge to save the world, the Joan/Julian duo also fought for their new-found happiness.

They were walking in the same park where Edith had first read the story about the disappearing hills. It was still March 2029, though so much had happened in the intervening days since the first sightings of Vanish. As Joan walked hand in hand with Julian looking at the little brook ambling down the uneven terrain and the spring flowers beginning to bloom, she thought about the famous cherry blossoms that she had never made time to visit. She turned to Julian and suggested they spend a day at the local cherry blossom festival that year if they and the world made it through this crisis.

It was late morning, and the March sun was strong and radiant in the sky. To Joan and Julian, it seemed to radiate not only light and heat, but hope as well. "Isn't it amazing" pondered Julian, "how the sun is an average star by standards in the universe, but to us it is our source of light and energy and so critical to life?"

"That reminds me," countered Joan, "we should also visit the planetarium and see the new shows about the sun, the stars, and the universe if we get a chance."

Drew was aware of the romance between his cousin and his colleague. He enjoyed having become friends with Joan and though he wished Joan well, he would have preferred it if she had chosen someone other than the cousin who had always been more popular than himself. He was struggling with his natural reluctance to see others happy and his new-found awareness of people that had been provoked by Julian's nightmarish experience near Nepal. He reminded himself about Julian's encounter with Vanish and admonished himself for his own pettiness. Part of him wondered if his own life would have been more fulfilled if he had disliked people less for so many years and opened up to them instead. Now with Vanish looming over them, Drew couldn't help but feel nostalgic about what might have been and happiness he may have missed.

The Drones Report Back

The drones had turned in the samples they had extracted from some of the affected zones. Results from detailed analysis put to rest the conjectures of disappearance and confirmed shrinking as the cause. The atoms and molecules in every sample examined were miniscule compared to normal. While individual structures and shapes were not retained, the samples studied confirmed that their atoms had indeed become smaller.

The news spread, broadcast through every news outlet and reverberating through social media. While it did not solve the problem or halt the effect, it did quell the competing theories and the world accepted that it was dealing with an incredible phenomenon of shrinking in select parts of the globe and maybe out in space too. This authentication enabled different groups to focus efforts to close in on Shrink as the perpetrator, and people hoped this would facilitate the search for solutions. The vocal protagonists of the various Vanish scenarios rapidly dispersed as scientific facts disproved their theories. Some reluctantly converted to join the Shrink congregation and others stayed in their little groups, shunned by those busy seeking solutions to Shrink.

Invoking the Higgs Model

The earlier discussions on muons and possible variations of the properties of electrons channeled to yet another particle: the Higgs boson. Predicted initially by theories that leaned on known symmetries of nature and the physics of particles and materials, the Higgs boson had been discovered in 2012 and had been much in the news at the time. Its own properties are determined by the state and the emptiness of the universe and it is connected to the amount of matter in everyday particles like electrons.

"Could the catastrophe somehow relate to an imbalance in the Higgs field and how electrons gain substance from it?" pondered JD, as he stood on the back porch and looked at the sky and the cosmos beyond. "Could it be some sort of weird quantum tunneling? Physicists have conjectured that our current universe could tunnel to a more stable state that would then change the world as we know it. The probability of this is so small we never worried about it. Maybe these incidences are like tunneling episodes before the entire universe succumbs?"

Similar questions were being asked by others around the globe. As occasionally happens, innovative ideas blossom in different minds and places, sometimes simultaneously. Scientific progress is often the convergence of multiple bold concepts cemented by knowledge and discoveries from the past. Most scientists battling Shrink had by now abandoned rigidity of views in favor of unknown answers. Traditional rules seemed to evaporate in the new and unexpected manifestations in the world of electrons and quantum physics. The global excitement revved up as creative questions and thoughts activated the communication channels.

Sipping a latte at the new coffee shop more than an ocean away in the Far East, Leela was posing similar questions to her friend and colleague: "Why would the Higgs field be perturbed and why would this affect only select electrons in select regions?"

"I have no answer" was the puzzled response. He attempted humor to lighten the fear: "Nothing spectacular has happened in our cosmic neighborhood recently, no exploding star in the vicinity or even a sudden flirting by a black hole."

JD Chats about the Higgs Field

Edith's living room was often the meeting place of their volunteer group and Eddie and Sarah's friends frequently stopped by. JD was in constant dialogue and discussions with fellow scientists round the world and the children hung on his every word. That evening, he had been wondering aloud about the Higgs field that was fixed in the primordial soup of the infant universe. In some sense, it defined the state of the universe and beyond. All these centuries it had lain dormant, with no sounding of its existence or presence. Why would it suddenly awaken and tamper with the properties of electrons, if indeed that is what it was doing? He tried to explain the Higgs particle and its manifestations to his usual captive audience of family and friends:

"The amount of matter in a subatomic particle like an electron or its "substance" as it were, is determined by how it responds to the Higgs field."

Eddie was amused. "What is the Higgs field? Is it like a football field?" he asked.

The question made JD ponder a bit. "Hmm. Not exactly," he responded. Choosing his words carefully, he continued: "The football field is on the surface of the earth. The Higgs field fills the universe and the Higgs boson the scientists detected is connected to it, or in some ways is a part of it. One might say the substance of a subatomic particle like an electron (or its weight in a sense) is determined by how it connects with Higgs field."

Sarah thought about the ball pits they sometimes

played in and shared the thought. "Is it like some people can move more easily in ball pits than others?" she asked.

"That's as good an analogy as any other," JD answered. He looked lovingly at his grandchildren and assembled family and resolved even more firmly to save them and the world.

As the family tried to understand the universe through JD's eyes, questions continued to fly around the world. Unfortunately, answers were missing. It was unknown and unchartered territory that the global conglomerate of scientists and non-scientists tried to traverse. No one could think what may have triggered the imbalance in nature and sporadic shifts in the electron mass, if these indeed were the trigger and the cause.

Can the World and Civilization Survive Shrink?

Time was flying and the Shrink was even more out of control by Day 8. The scientists and the technology gurus persevered even though standard systems and communications were beginning to fail. Spanning generations and disciplines, scientists worked as a team alongside stalwarts of technology and industry. Governments of countries large and small made available all resources that 2029 science and technology enterprise could offer. Volunteer groups like Edith's served as the glue easing communication barriers and plugging holes in global efforts as needed. The world watched as the scientific process of hypothesis and debunking continued in the search for solutions. Never had the scientific community been under such pressure to cooperate and to accelerate the path to results.

Whatever the cause, could Shrink be reversed or halted? There would be time for the whys if they survived. If not, no one would be left to know. The earth and all in it might shrink to become a tiny bubble in space or collapse into a miniature asteroid. This picture of doomsday or the end of the world had never been predicted by science or religion. The earth seemed to have selected from nowhere the most bizarre and strangest form of extinction.

Given the enormity of the challenge and the lack

of any definitive answers, humanity seized on the nebulous paths to solutions beginning to emerge. Most people by now agreed that somehow the Higgs field and the state of the universe had wobbled and this had caused the electrons to become heavy in some areas and shrink the atoms. The ray of opportunity here was the fact that the whole universe had not shifted but the imbalance was manifesting itself as quantum tunneling episodes in limited areas—just as they have been conjecturing. Based on this hypothesis, they explored possible actions that could perhaps attempt to restore balance in the universe so it could be rescued from the fluctuations.

Perhaps if the endangered regions could be stabilized, the entire universe might revert to its original state that made life possible for us in the first place. "Could we generate beams of Higgs bosons (discovered a couple of decades earlier)?" asked an enterprising and optimistic young scientist from Europe.

"Perhaps this would appease the Higgs field and readjust how it feeds the electrons," chimed in another. There was no technology available to try this, however. They would have to find a solution that could be implemented with available technology.

Muons to the Rescue?

Yet another novel idea began to emerge, looping back on earlier thoughts about muons. What if the affected areas were sprayed with muons? The muons would rapidly turn into electrons and there was a chance that the newly created electrons might escape the Higgs perturbation and would form new normal atoms. The idea encompassed the probability that the concentration of new electrons might also stop future Higgs field imbalances. This would only work if the turbulence in the Higgs field was confined to the affected regions and to existing electrons. It would require that the phenomenon spare new electrons born from the muons. It was by no means a perfect plan and had too many parts relying on optimism. But there were no other plans!

Suddenly, the world became intensely interested in the normally invisible muons flying around us. Leela had spent much of her life studying these ephemeral particles that live for fractions of a second on human time scales. She was happy to chat about muons via video with Sarah, Eddie, and their friends. "Muons shower upon us from space and often pass right through us," Leela explained. "Similar in many characteristics to the familiar electrons that build atoms, muons (sometimes called 'heavy electrons') live only for about two microseconds and then they turn into electrons and other particles."

"That is so sad," said Fiona, who was listening in with the children.

"Ah! But they can live longer when they are moving very fast," Leela laughed.

"Although the normal lifespan of a muon is about two microseconds, they live much longer when they are racing through space or the atmosphere and moving at very high speeds."

"Maybe I can use that when I encourage people to keep moving and running," said the fitness-expert side of Fiona. "People should learn from the muon and not lounge around but move about to live longer."

Sarah was listening avidly and she wanted to know

why muons live longer when moving fast. But Leela had to sign off for a meeting and she promised to share the story another day.

Assembling the Muon Army

Sarah, Eddie, and Fiona trooped out to the front lawn to find JD, who was on the phone talking about concentrated beams of muons. As he hung up, Eddie asked why people were talking about muon beams and muon generators if muons are already all around us.

"We can't control or manipulate the muons that come from space or are formed in the atmosphere," JD responded. "We want to be able to generate a whole lot of muons in one place so they will make a lot of electrons at the same time in close proximity to each other and maybe make the Higgs field stable again."

Fiona liked all kinds of nature analogies. "That reminds me of how clouds are scattered all around but they have to focus as rain clouds for rain to fall," she commented.

Eddie got the idea. "In the case of muons, we can't wait for them to gather together," he noted. "We have to generate them in a collected way," he concluded, seemingly having his own "Eureka" moment of understanding.

Trying to use muons to attempt to stabilize the universe seemed to be the only actionable path forward. Fortunately, 2029's Earth dwellers had reached a pinnacle in science and technology and had acquired a global scientific ethos that had promoted collaborative connections across the branches of science and technology and across nations. In this semi-utopian setting, sophisticated yet compact muon generators had recently been developed. Some of these were mobile, although they were few in number. The muons they made were used for various purposes that spanned basic research as well as diverse applications including tomography for archeology, materials testing, and security. Some of these muon generators were owned by governments and others by industry.

An effort was immediately launched to see how many mobile muon generators could be found or assembled. Speed was of the essence. Robots that were not affected by Vanish and were still functional were recruited along with the people who managed them to track down all high-intensity muon production devices that could be moved. Along with the rest of the world, Leela, Drew, Edith, Jake, and JD used their combined expertise to identify and round up mobile muon sources.

Amidst a rapidly dwindling population and at-risk geography, the saviors continued their efforts. Since the number of muon sources were limited, some mechanism would have to be put in place to determine where they should be deployed. This would be a new challenge to the world population to see if their leaders and some combination of scientists, engineers, and politicians could agree on the sites.

Making Decisions

Governments, agencies, and corporations around the world worked with the United Nations to plan the unleashing of the muons in affected areas. An obvious point of contention was deciding which locations would receive the muon treatment as they would not be able to attend to all affected sites. Some countries wanted to keep their muon sources for use in their affected neighborhoods. Multi-national corporations discussed their preferences with their shareholders. But people did not have time to argue and fight over the limited resources. There was too much at stake.

Those involved were able to agree to appoint a small committee with representatives from science, technology, government and industry with as much geographical representation as possible. Jake presented the results of the testing that proved the phenomenon they were combatting was shrinking and not disappearance. JD elucidated on the Higgs field and the theory of the day that it was tunneling out of its current state in select regions and affecting the properties of electrons and hence atoms. Leela explained about muons and how they decay into electrons and the current plan to deploy muon sources to create new electrons in selected areas. A technology expert presented a quick slide on the mobile muon sources and what they need to operate.

"What happens if we do nothing?" the chairperson asked.

"There is a tiny chance that the universe will stop these fluctuations on its own, just like they started," JD responded. "But can we take that chance?"

"Will it work?" asked a committee member.

"We can only hope," responded Leela. "We have no other plan."

"How many muon sources do we have?" asked another member.

"We have about ten, but two of them are small and should really be used in one place for maximum effect," answered one of the technology experts. "We should add there is a request from the company that owns one of these small sources to use it near their plant, where many records and equipment have been destroyed."

The committee deliberated behind closed doors, pouring over the world map that identified zones where Shrink had attacked. They chose the ones closest to habitation, holding on to hope that perhaps some of the people who had been lost could be recovered at some future time if the world made it through this crisis. They also took into account their proximity to muon sources so that transport to the sites would be easier and faster.

The committee gave the green light for the selected sites to be treated with concentrated muons. The portable muon generators were put in place and power sources hooked up. Acres of barren land stood mute witnesses to the distortion plague. Covered with the shrunken debris of buildings, trees, and aborted lives, hopes and aspirations, they silently mourned the past. Fountains of hope lay stoppered within the people left to try living.

The Countdown

The countdown began at noon on Day 12:

Five . . . four . . . three . . . two . . . one . . . zero.

There was no salute or sound for the muon saviors. There was no flash of brilliant light, no battle cry, or flares. Silent yet coordinated, the armies of muons were forced onto affected zones. Invisible to the naked eye, the billions of muons spewed out from the muon generators and decayed to create the new generations of concentrated electrons as planned.

Crucial questions remained unanswered: Were the diagnosis and the treatment mode the right ones? Would they work? Would they be saved from this disaster of epic proportions? Only time would tell. Would the new electrons born from the muons survive as normal electrons? Would they bond with the wandering nuclei to form atoms and molecules of normal size? Would the universe stop its random acts of tunneling to bubbles of new states where electrons were heavier?

People remaining watched anxiously as human ingenuity, technology, and the fruits of scientific research and innovation sought to save them. How beautiful was the world they lived in! Had they ever paused to ponder at how the Higgs field had to be just right to make them and their world as it was? Neither did they think about the awesome import of the right size of the sun, the right location of the earth, the right DNA structure, and so many other amazing facts of the universe. They did not marvel at how the precise properties of the electron gave size and dimension to matter and the known world. No, they had not cared or thought about these things. But they would do better. They would learn to love and cherish the planet and all in it. That is, if they made it.

Will it Work?

The rays of hope began to strengthen. Thankful for their lives, those remaining could not forget the lives lost. They faced too the desolation of a destroyed world, akin to the aftermath of a devastating war. Millions had been annihilated. People, habitation, and industry had been wiped out over vast areas. But those left would rebuild their lives and together they would win again if Shrink was aborted. And this time they would not let greed and the passion for immediate gratification blind them to nature, knowledge, and their confluence.

Edith, her family, and friends, along with the remaining people vowed that if they made it to the future they would join forces to rebuild their lives. They vowed allegiance to understanding and appreciating existence. They would make the earth and its environment a beautiful and friendly place.

"I will not take electrons for granted anymore," commented JD. "We rely on them to make most of our technology and daily lives work, from computer chips inside our smart phones to communications and so much more. Yet we mostly ignored them until the universe played with their properties!"

Sarah was sitting next to him. "They are part of us, too? Right?" she asked.

"Indeed. Every atom in our bodies and the objects around us have electrons and we need them to stay just the way they are," JD gratefully confirmed.

Fifteen minutes had elapsed since the countdown. It was too soon to tell. Would it or wouldn't it work? Thirty minutes. Did they dare to smile? Had the release of the muons and the new-born electrons averted the crisis? Had the Higgs and its interaction with electrons stabilized? Fear and anticipation persisted. Drained by the trauma of the Shrink, they pledged to make tomorrow more meaningful—if they survived. Would they succeed in rescuing 2029 and its progeny from the jaws of the annihilating Shrink? Apprehensive, agonized, yet stimulated by hope, they all waited.

Saved—for Now

An hour passed with no new reports of disappearance. People began to breathe again, but slowly. It was not over. They did not know if the muons and the new generation of electrons had saved the world. Would they need another shot? They hoped not, for the Shrink had debilitated power sources and a repeat of the coordinated muon release would be hard. The global population had achieved an impossible feat in coming together to try to save the world and its cosmic environment. Whether it would work was yet to be proved.

All over the world people were waiting and watching, thankful for every moment they lived. Those who had lost loved ones to episodes of Shrink silently honored their memories. Industry and governments with offices in affected regions had lost data and equipment that would not be recovered and hoped that their data back-up systems would help find customer data at least.

If they made it, there would be no way to tell for sure if the universe and the Higgs field had just reverted back to their normal states or if it was indeed their human efforts and the muons that saved them. They would never know exactly what had triggered the shift or whether it was truly the muons and new electrons that stabilized them back to normalcy. What was important was that electrons remain their normal selves so that our world can stay the way it is and be compatible for life.

As people counted every second that passed and brought them closer to safety, they were also excruciatingly aware of the enormous amount of rebuilding that would have to be done to the planet. But humanity would persevere and make new developments. Their children would grow up to discover new possibilities and chart their own paths to the future.

It had all happened so fast! It had been twelve days of a horror movie getting worse every day. It was even more remarkable that the world had come together in the short spate of these agonizing twelve days and put in place an emergency response. Leaders in every country thanked their citizens and workforce, and in particular the science and technology professionals for their roles and contributions in saving the world. They hoped the empathy and cooperation would continue and recognized the impact people can have when they work together for a shared cause.

Looking Forward

Edith and her family stayed up all night, waiting with increasing hope as the earth rotated to meet sunrise and the new day. They were even closer than before because of what they had gone through and how close Shrink had crept to Edith and Fiona. Edith turned to Jake and thanked him for making the drone-based research happen. Jake in turn acknowledged how Sarah and Eddie had inspired him to take action. JD smiled with a mixture of amazement and wonder that they had accomplished what they did. He marveled too about how the universe can throw us a curve ball at any time!

People in Edith's orbit and elsewhere were returning to their lives. Leela would be flying back to the U.S. later that day as flights were expected to resume. Joan and Julian would be stopping by soon to join the family for breakfast. Poignantly reminiscent of her traumatic encounter with Shrink, Edith wanted to help everyone she could. She picked up the phone and told Joan that they were welcome to bring Drew if he wanted to come over too.

The volunteer group Edith, her colleagues, and friends had assembled would have much to do in the coming days and months as would all the people who had escaped Shrink. The global concerted effort to save the world would serve as inspiration for generations to come. Perhaps they will never know for sure if the universe had realigned itself solely due to the release of the muons or it had just stopped wobbling as randomly as it had started. But their success with disparate groups of people working together for the greater good would live on.

The world deserved a day off to celebrate its freedom from Shrink and the plan was to dedicate the following day to those who had been lost. Today, they would be thankful and enjoy the simple things of life and the beautiful spring day that almost did not arrive.

As Edith and her extended family trooped into the kitchen for waffles and coffee, birds chirped and sunshine beckoned them outdoors. The back porch had enough seating for them to sit together and enjoy the little pleasures like breakfast as they welcomed their new leases on life.

JD paused at the doorway on his way to the porch, gratefully absorbing the normalcy of the moment and his happy family. His gaze took in the trees and the sky, and his thoughts moved beyond the visible horizon to the magnificence of the cosmos and its profound mysteries. His heart bled for those who had shrunk and were lost to society. He leaned on hope and chance that they might perhaps be living new miniature lives in another universe with a different Higgs field. He reflected on how much Sarah and Eddie loved science and felt heartened about their generation. Sipping his coffee, he joined the family outdoors, looking forward to the next generation storming the unknown, and ensuring the safety of our earth and our universe.

Closing Note

"Where Did the Hills Go?" is a science-inspired fictional story, set in the future. As with historical fiction, there are some elements of facts that inspire the fiction. Here are a few . . .

Our current universe *may* exist in an unstable state, and there *might* be a possibility (albeit very, *very* minute) that it could shift to a more stable state. *However, the manifestation of this effect and its fantasized resolution in the novella are completely fictional.*

The Higgs field is associated with the state of the universe and the vacuum and does determine the mass (or substance) of most elementary particles like electrons. *However, the fictional increases in the masses of electrons in certain regions—portrayed as resulting from the shift in the state of the universe and the Higgs field, are illusory and imaginary.*

Muons are elementary particles that generally decay in microseconds into electrons. Muonic atoms (where muons replace electrons) are much smaller than regular atoms, and yet, real. Muons do shower on us in the atmosphere. They can also be made in large accelerators, *but we do not have portable muon generators as of now.*

Science facts and explanations elucidated by JD, Leela, and others are correct, *but the situation, solution, events, and characters are entirely fictitious.*

CPSIA information can be obtained
at www.ICGtesting.com
Printed in the USA
BVHW01s0051290418
514135BV00040BA/218/P